The Emperor's New Clothes

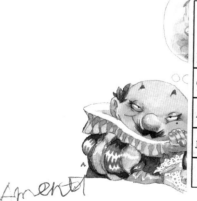

Barrie Wade and O'Kif

W

For Bethany, Eva and Emma Joy – B.W.

1
A Vain Emperor

Once there lived a vain emperor who loved to show off in new clothes. He spent hours every day trying on new outfits and admiring himself in the mirror.

One day, two weavers came to his palace. They took off their hats and bowed to the Emperor. "We are expert weavers," said one. "We can weave you the best cloth in the world to make the finest robes anyone has ever seen."

"For a clever emperor like you, there is something quite special about our weaving," said the other. "Our beautiful cloth is so fine that stupid people cannot even see it."

"That's fantastic," said the Emperor. "There is a royal procession next week and I want to wear the grandest robes ever made."
He pictured himself striding down the street with all eyes on him and everyone admiring him greatly.

The vain Emperor gave the weavers a bag full of gold and a room in the palace, where they could make the new robes. The cheating weavers took their weaving and sewing tools in with them and pretended to work. Scissors snipped and needles stitched through the air.

2
The Special Cloth

Out in the street, notices told the people that there would be a procession in a week's time. Everyone wondered what the Emperor would wear for the occasion. The royal maid heard the people talking about the procession and making guesses about the Emperor's clothes.

"I can tell you a secret," she said. "This royal procession will be the most amazing anyone has ever seen and the Emperor will look stunning. The weavers are making a special cloth for him. It is so fine that stupid people cannot see it," she told them.

The Emperor was so excited. He could hardly
wait for the weavers to finish their work,
so he sent his Prime Minister to see them.
"Look at the splendid colours!" said
one weaver.

The Prime Minister looked hard to see what the weavers were showing him.

"Look at the beautiful pattern!" said the other weaver.

The Prime Minister could not see anything, but he did not want to seem stupid.

The Prime Minister went back to the Emperor, smiling. "I have never seen anything so amazing," he reported. "What splendid colours! What a beautiful pattern!"

The Emperor pictured himself wearing rich, luxurious robes in the procession next day and he too smiled. He wanted to show the weavers how pleased he was with their work, so he sent them another bag overflowing with gold.

Later that same day, the excited Emperor was again dying to know if his new cloth was ready. So he sent his Chancellor to see how the weavers were getting on.

"Let me see what you have done so far," ordered the Chancellor.
They smiled and held their arms out to show him. "Look at the lovely colours! Look at the marvellous patterns!" said the cheating weavers.

15

The Chancellor looked hard and carefully, but he could not see anything either. However, he did not want to admit he was stupid. So when he went back to report to the Emperor, he bowed and smiled.

"I have seen something truly wonderful,"
he said. "What lovely colours. What a
marvellous pattern!"

The vain Emperor imagined himself dressed
in a lovely, marvellous outfit. He was full of
gratitude, so he gave the weavers another
bag of gold.

3
The Emperor's Robes

It was hard for the impatient Emperor to wait. He was burning to see the results of all the hard work. At last, however, the weavers carried the finished cloth to the Emperor.

He was waiting, sitting on his throne.
On one side of him stood the Chancellor.
On the other side stood the Prime Minister.
"Look at the marvellous pattern!" said the
Chancellor.
"Look at the splendid colours!" said the
Prime Minister.

Both the Chancellor and the Prime Minister seemed happy that the Emperor would look wonderful in the procession. The Prime Minister helped to show him the finished cloth. The Emperor looked down from his throne, but he could not see anything. However, he did not want to seem stupid. "How magnificent!" he said. "This is just what I want."

The royal procession was the next day.
There was little time left, so the cheating
weavers went back into their work room.
They pretended to cut and sew the new cloth
into robes fit for the Emperor.

Royal
procession
tomorrow

At last they cried: "Our work is done! The Emperor's new clothes are ready. Let us see how he looks in them."

The Emperor came in and took off all his clothes. The weavers had a mirror ready for the fitting session and the Emperor stood up in front of it. Then the weavers pretended to dress him in his new robes, smiling happily all the time.

"Come and see my new robes," cried the
Emperor. He stood, waiting to be admired.
"A perfect fit!" all his ministers cried. They
could not see anything, but nobody wanted
to seem stupid.

Everybody said how wonderful and elegant
the Emperor looked in his new clothes and
they gave him all their attention. The
cheating weavers quickly left with the gold.

4
The Royal Procession

Next day was a holiday for the royal
procession and all the people came to
watch. The Emperor walked proudly in
the procession with his ministers.

Along the streets, all the people cheered.
"What a magnificent robe! What an elegant
suit! What lovely new clothes!" they cried.
They could not see anything either, but
nobody wanted to appear stupid.

The crowd looked on happily, enjoying the procession. Suddenly, a child pointed, yelling: "Look at the Emperor. He has got nothing on!"

"That's right!" the people shouted. "He's got nothing on!"

Everyone laughed and their laughter rang in the Emperor's ears. At last, he realised he was walking in the procession without a stitch of clothing on. The vain Emperor blushed and felt very, very stupid.

About the story

The Emperor's New Clothes is a European fairy tale. It was written by Hans Christian Andersen and was published in 1837 with another tale he had written: *The Little Mermaid*. The story is based on one originally included in the *Libro de los ejemplos (Tales of Count Lucanor,* 1335), a medieval Spanish collection with various sources, by Juan Manuel, Prince of Villena.

Hans Christian Andersen was born in Denmark in 1805. He wrote plays, travel books, novels and poems, but he is best remembered for his fairy tales. He decided very late to change the ending of *The Emperor's New Clothes* to include the child crying out that the Emperor was nude.

Be in the story!

Imagine you are the weavers and you have just run from the palace. How do you feel about the Emperor?

Now imagine you are the Emperor. How do you feel about being so worried about your new clothes? What would you like to say to the weavers and your ministers?

Franklin Watts
First published in Great Britain in 2016 by The Watts Publishing Group

Series Editor: Jackie Hamley
Series Advisor: Catherine Glavina
Series Designer: Cathryn Gilbert

A CIP catalogue record for this book is available
from the British Library.

The artwork for this story first appeared in
Hopscotch Fairy Tales: The Emperor's New Clothes

ISBN 978 1 4451 4657 7 (hbk)
ISBN 978 1 4451 4658 4 (library ebook)
ISBN 978 1 4451 4659 1 (pbk)

Printed in China

Franklin Watts
An imprint of
Hachette Children's Group
Part of The Watts Publishing Group
Carmelite House
50 Victoria Embankment
London EC4Y 0DZ

An Hachette UK Company
www.hachette.co.uk

www.franklinwatts.co.uk

FSC
www.fsc.org
MIX
Paper from
responsible sources
FSC® C104740